For my brothers, Derek and Christopher, who came with the
terror-tory – from Wendy with love.

For Jess who is learning to say 'Diplodocus' and other wonderful
words – from Niki with love.

1 3 5 7 9 10 8 6 4 2

Copyright© text Wendy Hartmann and Niki Daly 1996
Copyright© illustrations Niki Daly 1996

Wendy Hartmann and Niki Daly have asserted their
rights under the Copyright, Designs and Patents Act, 1988 to be
identified as the author and illustrator of this work.

First published in the United Kingdom 1996
by The Bodley Head Children's Books
Random House, 20 Vauxhall Bridge Road, London SW1V 2SA

Random House Australia (Pty) Limited
20 Alfred Street, Milsons Point, Sydney,
New South Wales 2061, Australia

Random House New Zealand Limited
18 Poland Road, Glenfield,
Auckland 10, New Zealand

Random House South Africa (Pty) Limited
PO Box 337, Bergvlei 2012, South Africa

Random House UK Limited Reg. No. 954009

A CIP record for this book is available from the British Library

ISBN 0 370 322 738

Printed in Hong Kong

The DINOSAURS Are Back
And it's all your fault Edward!

Story by
Wendy Hartmann & Niki Daly
Pictures by Niki Daly

The Bodley Head

London

"Edward?"

"*Mmmm?*"

"What if that rock under your bed isn't a rock at all...? What if it's an egg, Edward?"

"Huuuh!"

"What if it's a DINOSAUR EGG...?"

"... and it hatches, Edward?"

"It'll eat like a dustbin.

And SOMEBODY will have to change its nappy.

"It'll need potty-training, Edward."

"As it grows up you'll have to teach it good manners."

"And how to behave when Aunty Vi comes around.

You'll have to take it for walkies.

"What if it follows you to school, Edward?

And wants to go everywhere you go...

and do everything you do?

It'll be just like a shadow, Edward."

"You'll have to watch it every moment of the day…

and night, Edward."

"Dinosaurs sleep at night, stupid!"

"Edward, EDWARD!"

"What?"

"Not when there's a big, crazy moon.

"A big, crazy moon makes Dinosaurs REALLY mad, Edward.

So mad that they forget who their friends are.

"They run wild,
looking for their mother and father.

Hollering for their brothers and sisters...
cousins, aunts and uncles...
Howling for their big grandaddy...

"The King of the Dinosaurs."

"Then they go looking for little boys who steal Dinosaur eggs!"

"They drag the little egg-stealer, kicking and screaming, right out of bed!"